Ralph THE Magic Rabbit

RALPH THE MAGIC RABBIT

Adam Frost

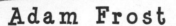

Illustrated by
Henning Löhlein

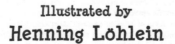

MACMILLAN CHILDREN'S BOOKS

First published 2005 by Macmillan Children's Books
a division of Macmillan Publishers Ltd
20 New Wharf Road, London N1 9RR
Basingstoke and Oxford
Associated companies throughout the world
www.panmacmillan.com

ISBN 1 405 05043 8

To my family
A.F.

. . . and to mine
H.L.

Chapter One

It was the middle of spring, and all the animals in the forest were singing. The birds were warbling in the trees, the crickets were chirping in the fields and, in a secluded hollow, a colony of snails was halfway through its first song of the morning.

Oh, being a snail is a wonderful thing!
All that we do is eat flowers and sing.
We live under hedges and boulders and bricks
And hide in our shells when we're prodded
    with sticks.
Our powers of suction are pretty incredible.
In France, we're regarded as perfectly edible.

But there was one snail who wasn't joining in. Sid the Snail had crawled under a bush, then crawled under a stone and then crawled inside his shell.

'I don't see what's so great about being a snail,' he said, his voice echoing inside his shell. 'Everything takes so long long long. If I want to go to a New Year's Eve party, I have to set off on August the thirteenth thirteenth thirteenth. If someone taps me on the shoulder, by the time I turn round they're usually dead dead dead. Nothing is as slow as I am am am.'

4

Then someone knocked three times on his shell. It was Sid's friend Baz the Beetle.

'Are you coming out?' Baz asked.

'No,' said Sid.

'Why not?' asked Baz.

'Because I'm sick of being alive,' Sid said.

'Why? What's wrong with it?' Baz asked.

'I'm not fast enough,' said Sid. 'I want to be faster than a speeding bullet or a flash of lightning.'

'Oh, OK,' Baz said, and went to find someone else's shell to knock on.

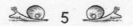

After half an hour of sulking, Sid emerged from his shell. It was like toothpaste being squeezed out of a tube, or jam leaking out of the side of a sandwich.

Sid sighed and slowly looked around. And at that moment across the clearing he saw a snail with a shower-cap on and a towel balanced on top of his shell. The snail headed towards a hollow tree-trunk and disappeared inside. Sid was curious and decided to follow him.

When Sid got to the tree-trunk, an earwig appeared in front of the entrance and crossed four of its six arms.

'All right, slowcoach. You know the rules. One in, one out,' he said.

Sid saw a sign nailed to the tree.

HARRY'S HEALTH CLUB
The insect gym
For her and him
Thursdays: SNAILS ONLY

'Hey,' Sid thought to himself, 'this place might help me to go faster.'

So when a blotchy, panting snail came out, Sid went in.

The tree-trunk was a hive of activity. There was a large puddle in which three snails were swimming lengths. A lifeguard ant sat on top of a mushroom and blew a whistle every time anyone tried to do widths. One snail had just got out of the shallow end and was drying his shell with a lettuce leaf.

On Sid's left, other snails were exercising. One snail had balanced three acorns on each of his feelers; another was being stretched by two fleas (fleas were fitness experts) and another was trying to uproot a thistle.

'Wow,' Sid said aloud, 'this place is perfect.'

Sid approached
an old snail
with a squelchy
face who was
resting by
the puddle. He looked like
he'd been using the gym for years.

'Excuse me, I'd like to increase my
speed,' Sid said. 'Which exercise
should I do first?'

'Hmm,' the old snail said, 'you
could try flinging conkers.'

'And will that do any good?' Sid
asked.

'Er, no, not good as such,' said
the old snail, 'in fact, you'll feel awful.
But if you repeat the exercise three
times a day for five years,

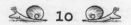 10

you'll begin to notice a slight
improvement.'

'A slight improvement!' Sid
exclaimed. 'But I want to be faster
than a speeding bullet or a
flash of lightning.'

The old
snail sighed.
'I don't see
how you're going to manage that.
You're a snail. A dollop of slop with a
seashell on your back. You're not
exactly designed for bounding through
the fields.'

'But do I have to be this slow?'
Sid asked.

'Sorry, that's nature for you,'
the old snail replied.

'Look, there's a mad-scientist snail who lives in the next tree along. He might have some ideas. I'm afraid I have to go now and balance on an onion for two hours.'

Sid said goodbye politely and oozed towards the exit.

When Sid got outside, he blinked as his eyes readjusted to the light. Then, looking to his left, he saw another hollowed-out tree.

'I think I should pay that mad-scientist snail a visit,' he said to himself.

It took Sid half an hour to get there, during which time he noticed a trail of bright green smoke pouring from the entrance to the tree-trunk. As Sid got closer, he couldn't help noticing that it smelt of Stilton cheese.

Sid put his head inside the tree. 'Hello?' he said. There was no reply. 'Hello?' he said again. Sid took a deep breath and slid inside.

Through the smoke, Sid made out a snail with a white moustache, sitting behind a table built from tree-bark. The snail had a mouse's skeleton hanging up next to him, and lumps of chalk on a ledge above his head. A pile of dazed ants lay on the table in front of him.

'Ah, another guinea pig,' said the scientist.

Sid looked confused. 'I always thought I was a snail.'

'Just sign here, here and here,' said the scientist. Like most snails, he had two pairs of feelers. His eyes were on the end of his long pair, and he used his short pair like hands to move things around. He gave Sid a form with his short feelers. Sid read:

I, the undersigned, allow Professor Snail Q. Snail to singe, pummel, perforate, bury and shred me in the name of science.

Sid replied
quickly.
'Look, I've
only come
here because
I want to go faster.'

'Faster? Oh, I see,' said the mad
scientist. 'I'm so sorry. My mistake.'
He told Sid to sit down on a pile of
dock-leaves.

'I need your help,' said Sid. 'I was
wondering if you had some kind of
potion to make me speedier.'

The mad scientist gave his feelers
a twirl. 'I suppose I could cook up
some martlet and grebe juice.'

'And will that make me go faster?'
asked Sid.

'No, it will make your head and your tail change places,' said the mad scientist.

'Hmm. I was sort of more interested in something to make me faster,' said Sid.

'In that case,' said the mad scientist, 'you could try some Tungo Powder.' He lifted up an acorn-cup full of yellow powder from under the table.

'And will that increase my speed?' asked Sid.

'No. Rub three grains on to your forehead and you'll turn into a King Edward potato. Watch.' He picked up an ant from the table and demonstrated.

'Impressive,' said Sid when it was over, 'but I'm still really taken with the "speed" idea.'

'Well, how about a Thunderclap Hat?' the mad scientist asked. He produced a cap made of a broken eggshell and two sprigs of heather.

'And what will that do?' asked Sid.

'Try it on and see,' said the mad scientist.

'No, no, just tell me,' said Sid.

'Your shell will burst into flames.'

'Look,' snapped Sid, 'I don't want to catch fire, or grow wings, or anything like that. I just want to be the fastest animal ever.'

'OK, OK,' said the scientist, giving a deep sigh. 'I'm afraid it can't be done. Scientifically speaking, snails are like dribble or sweat. They trickle. They ooze. Ask the Three Wise Snails if you don't believe me.'

'The Three Wise Snails?'

'Yes, they live on the rock opposite. I've been trying to get them to volunteer for experiments since last November.'

Now, Sid had heard of the Three Wise Snails. They were consulted every time any of the forest snails had a problem. Whereas most snails had a head and a tail, the Three Wise Snails had a head and another head. They had six heads between three snails. This made them twice as clever as every other snail in the wood.

When Sid heard they were close by, he said goodbye to the mad scientist and left the tree-trunk at what was (for him) a brisk pace.

As Sid got steadily closer to the Three Wise Snails, he began to make out the words of a song.

Oh, we're so clever and we're so wise.

Our brains are twice their natural size.

We can do the trickiest sums

With no assistance from our mums.

We found spelling tests enthralling

Before we even started crawling.

Although it's rude to brag or crow,

There's truly nothing we don't know.

Sid arrived just as they had
finished singing the song for the
sixth time.

He looked up at the three shells
with a head at each end silhouetted
against the sky.

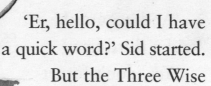

'Er, hello, could I have a quick word?' Sid started.

But the Three Wise Snails had fallen silent.

'Er, have you got a minute?' Sid began.

But there was still no answer.

'ARE YOU DEAF OR SOMETHING?' Sid shouted.

'No,' said one of the heads, 'but first you have to fawn.'

'Fawn?' Sid asked.

'Yes, fawn – flatter,' said the second head. 'Like, "O Wise Snails, you are so wise and kind . . ." That sort of thing.'

'Oh, OK,' said Sid. 'O Wise Snails, you are so wise and kind and powerful –'

'And beautiful,'
said a third head.

'Yes, don't forget
beautiful,' said the
first head.

'And beautiful,'
continued Sid, 'and
generous and mysterious.'

'OK, OK, that's enough, now what
do you want?' asked the first head.

'What about diaphanous?' said
a fourth head. 'He didn't say
diaphanous.'

'Shut up, Clive,' said the first head.
'We're not remotely diaphanous.
It means translucent or see-through.
Now, young snail, what do you
wish to ask?'

'I was wondering –' began Sid.

'Hang on, hang on,' said the first head. 'Assume the posture of universal deference and respect.'

'What do you mean?' Sid asked.

'Long feelers down, short feelers up, tail tucked into shell.'

'OK,' Sid said and assumed the correct position. 'Now, I was wondering –'

'Just a minute,' said the first head.
'Where's our present?'

'What present?' asked Sid.

'You can't expect us to listen to
your question unless you offer us
some kind of gift,' said the first head.

Sid saw a pebble next to him.
He picked it up and handed it over.
'Will this do?' he asked.

'We accept your offering of a precious stone,' said the first head, 'given in acknowledgement of our brainpower and learnedness. Now, what seems to be the problem?'

'Right,' said Sid, 'I was wondering if you knew how to make me fast.'

'Fast? What do you mean?' said the second head.

'I mean, like, twenty or thirty miles an hour,' said Sid.

'But you can't! You're a snail!' said the third head.

The fifth and the sixth heads began to titter.

'But I was hoping that with your intelligence and learnedness and all that other stuff that you might know how,' said Sid.

'My dear boy,' said the second head, 'the only way that you could go at that kind of speed would be inside the stomach of a peregrine falcon.'

The third head sniggered.

'But – bu –' stammered Sid.

'No more buts,' said the first head. 'We're the Three Wise Snails, not Ralph the Magic Rabbit.'

The other five heads all chuckled.

'Ralph the Magic Rabbit?' asked Sid.

'Ralph the Magic Rabbit. It's a joke,' said the first head.

'Why is it a joke?' asked Sid.

'Because Ralph the Magic Rabbit doesn't exist. He's an imaginary creature that supposedly lives at the other end of the forest. Only foolish old snails believe in him.'

'What does he do?'

'He's supposed to grant you your dearest wish.'

'Then I must find him,' said
Sid quietly.

'I've told you, he's not real,' said
the first head. 'He's like a fairy, or
a ghost.'

Sid had already started to
turn round.

'Wait a minute. Before leaving us
you must rotate thrice, say, "I thank
you," in Latin and curtsy before our
vegetable shrine,' the first head said,
nodding towards a few mouldy-
looking lumps at the base of
the rock.

But Sid didn't hear him.

Chapter Two

Sid was heading north, towards the other end of the forest. After two hours of travelling, he recognized an old grey beech tree with dark red leaves. This was the furthest he had ever travelled before. Once he passed that beech tree, he would no longer be on familiar soil.

He was about to
crawl forwards when a
bundle of sticks landed
in front of him followed
by an unhappy-looking robin.

'Bob!' exclaimed Sid. 'What are you
doing here?'

Bob the Wobbly Robin was famous
for being the most accident-prone
bird in the forest (apart from Chuck
the Unlucky Duck and Mark the
Disastrous Lark). He was always
losing his balance and falling on top
of passers-by.

'Oh, hello, Sid,' Bob said. 'I've
spent the whole week trying to build
a nest. I've not had much luck
though.'

'How come?' Sid asked.

'Well, first of all I built one in a cedar tree over by the lake,' Bob began, 'but the next day a couple of lumberjacks sawed the tree down. The day after, I built a new nest in a gooseberry bush next to the river, but the river flooded that night and I was lucky not to drown. The three nests after that were blown away in a gale, eaten by termites and sat on by a pig.'

'And what about just now?' Sid asked.

'A pine cone fell from the branch above me.

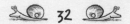

Completely knocked me for six,' Bob said. 'But what about you, Sid? You don't usually venture out this far.'

'I know,' said Sid, 'but I've got to get to the other end of the forest.'

'What?' Bob said. 'But that's miles away. It would take me all day to get there. It'll take you months.'

'I realize that,' Sid said, 'but I'm going anyway.'

'Well, I hope you know what you're doing,' said Bob. 'God knows I don't.' And with that he flew off with a twig in his beak.

Sid kept travelling for another half an hour, and then the sun set. He decided to crawl inside his shell and get some rest. He had a long day ahead of him tomorrow.

For a few minutes after Sid fell asleep, the forest was quiet and still. Then there was a snuffling sound, which turned into a shuffling sound, which soon turned into a scuffling, rustling, bustling sound. Three slugs appeared from under a pile of leaves. Three more were crawling over a tree stump. Within minutes, slugs were pouring out of every hedge, bush and tree in sight. There must have been thirty or forty of them, and they were all heading for Sid.

In Sid's part of the forest there weren't any slugs, so he had never been warned away from them. He didn't know that they spent every night of their lives hunting for sleeping snails. When they found one, they yanked its head forward and ripped its shell off. The snail was now a slug.

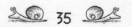 35

As the slugs closed in on Sid, they began to chant in low voices.

> Why should snails have all the fun?
>
> They have shells while we have none
>
> So we'll hunt down every one
>
> And never rest until it's done.

Sid felt the ground trembling and woke up, emerging sleepily from his shell. When he saw thirty slugs bearing down on him, he guessed that they weren't trying to make friends.

He started to move away as quickly as he could. One of the slugs shouted, 'Charge!' and the chase began. Neither Sid nor the slugs had ever moved so fast. Sid covered two inches in five minutes, the slugs covered two and a half inches; Sid managed four inches in the next ten minutes, but the slugs managed four and a half; Sid accelerated to half an inch a minute, but the slugs accelerated to three-quarters of an inch. Then, just as he felt their feelers tickling his tail, Sid sped up to an inch a minute, and the slugs gradually dropped away.

When he was alone again, Sid crawled behind a tree to get his breath back. 'They were out to get me all right,' he said to himself. 'I'm going to have to start hiding at night-time.'

He found a pile of stones and crawled underneath them. He was trembling so much it took him over an hour to get to sleep. Every time he closed his eyes he saw a giant slug, rearing up on its tail and opening its mouth wide.

The following morning Sid was still nervous, so he decided to sing a cheerful song.

I could get eaten,
Squashed or beaten,
Kicked against a tree.
But I don't mind,
I'm not the kind
Who gives up easily.

A bird might peck
Me through the neck
And feed me to her chicks.
But you know me,
I'll wriggle free
And stab them all with sticks.

Perhaps I'll stroll
Into a hole
Where snakes and lizards thrive.
But that's OK,
I'll crawl away
Half-eaten but alive.

After he had sung the song three times Sid felt a little better, although he still jumped every time a twig snapped in the bushes.

A little further into the forest, Sid came to a stream with a log lying across it. At one end of the log, a mouse was hunched over with his eyes shut. Sid slowly made his way towards the mouse.

'Hello!' Sid said when he arrived.

'Whooo!' the mouse shrieked. 'You scared the life out of me.'

'Really?' Sid replied.

'Yes, you did. You could have been a hawk or a hedgehog or anything. You shouldn't creep up on people like that.'

'Sorry, I was going as fast as I could,' said Sid. He looked up at the log. 'Anyway, what are you trying to do?'

'I've got to cross this stream,' said the mouse, 'but it's so hard.'

'Why?' asked Sid.

'Because anything could happen,' said the mouse. 'I could fall off, the wind might blow me away, the log could split in two . . .'

'I suppose,' said Sid.

'I could fall in the water and drown,' continued the mouse, 'or get swept out to sea, or get eaten by a heron.'

'Well, I'm going this way too,' said Sid, 'so shall I go first?' After the slugs, this didn't scare Sid at all.

'Fine by me,' said the mouse, and stepped aside.

Sid slid along the log, with the mouse shivering and squeaking behind him. When they got to the other side, the mouse nearly fainted with relief.

'We did it!' cried the mouse in disbelief. 'We're still in one piece.'

Sid gave the mouse a curious look and said, 'Tell me. Why did you want to cross that stream in the first place?'

'Because I'm going to the other end of the forest,' said the mouse.

Now it was Sid's turn to look surprised. 'Really? That's where I'm going. Why are you going to the other end of the forest?'

'Because I'm going to see Ralph the Magic Rabbit,' said the mouse.

'But – but –' Sid stammered, 'that's who I'm going to see. Only – I wasn't sure he existed.'

'Of course he exists,' said the mouse, 'and he's going to make me as strong as an ox. Then I won't be frightened any more.'

'So – what are you frightened of now?' asked Sid, looking at the mouse, who was twice his size.

'Oh, you name it really,' said the mouse. 'Loud noises, quiet noises, trees, rocks, other mice, clouds, blossom, snow, any animal bigger than me, any animal smaller than me, any animal the same size as me, the colour blue . . .'

Blue?

'Blue?'

'But when Ralph the Magic Rabbit
makes me the strongest mouse in the
world, I won't be scared of anything.
I'll be able to balance boulders on my
nose, I'll be able to throw donkeys up
trees, I'll be able to uproot bushes
with my tail.

'But wait a minute – did you say you were going to see Ralph the Magic Rabbit?'

'Yes,' said Sid.

'But it'll take you years,' said the mouse. 'Climb on my back and we'll go together.'

Sid thought about it for a moment, then climbed on.

'My name's Martin the Mouse,' said the mouse.

'I'm Sid the Snail,' said Sid.

Chapter Three

'**T**his is great,' Sid thought to himself as Martin scampered over logs, jumped over ditches and slunk through caves. 'I'll be at the other end of the forest in no time.'

They were about to cross an enormous poppy field when Martin sniffed the air. 'Squirrels,' he said.

He sniffed
the air again.
'Two of them.'
He sniffed the air
for a third time.
'They're fighting
each other. We'd
better steer clear.'

'Why?' asked Sid.

'Because squirrels are cold-blooded
killers who won't stop until they've
destroyed every living thing on the
planet.'

'Squirrels?' asked Sid.

'Or is it cows?' Martin thought
aloud, twitching his whiskers.

'I think we'll be all right,' said Sid.
'Let's keep going.'

They soon reached a clearing, in which two squirrels were standing either side of an acorn. They had their hands on their hips and their chins stuck out.

'I'm sorry, Tarquin,' said the squirrel on the left, 'but I saw it first.'

'I'm sorry, Terence,' said the squirrel on the right, 'but I got here first.'

'I saw it first,' said Terence the Squirrel, 'and that makes it my nut.'

'I got here first,' said Tarquin the Squirrel, 'and that makes it my nut.'

'Well, if it's your nut,' said Terence, 'why hasn't it got your name on it?'

'I don't know,' said Tarquin. 'Maybe because you rubbed it off.'

'You're that far away from a punch on the nose,' said Terence.

'I'll knock your block off, you young ruffian,' said Tarquin.

Terence picked up the nut and scrambled up the nearest tree. He scuttled up the trunk and bounded along one of the branches. Tarquin was hot on his trail, never losing sight of Terence for an instant.

When Terence tripped over a bird's nest, Tarquin caught up with him and grabbed the nut. Now it was Tarquin's turn to be chased. He ran down the tree, up another tree, sped along a branch, leaped off the end and landed on another branch.

Sid and Martin could only stop and stare as the treetops shook and rustled.

'Look at them fighting,' Martin said. 'I wish I was as strong and brave as that.'

'Look at them running,' Sid said. 'I wish I was that fast.'

They watched some more, both lost in their own thoughts.

'Hey,' Sid said finally, 'they're not in our way any more.'

'That's true,' said Martin. 'Let's get out of here.'

Martin scuttled forwards and Sid clung on.

'Why does Ralph the Magic Rabbit have to live so far away?' Sid asked.

'I was just thinking the same thing myself,' replied Martin.

The two animals pressed on till nightfall, pausing only to watch a sheep-courtship dance.

'What are they doing?' Sid asked.

'This is what sheep have to do if they want to get married,' explained Martin.

Two sheep were standing in a clearing. They stared

at each other for about ten minutes.
Then the male sheep (or ram) said,
'Baa!' The female sheep (or ewe) said,
'Baa!' The ram bowed to the ewe and
the ewe bowed to the ram. Then they
rotated 360 degrees until they were
facing each other again.

They jumped up and down on
the spot for thirty seconds. Then
the ram began to sing in a gentle,
crooning voice.

> You may be a sheep, but I love you.
>
> I love you so desperately.
>
> You may have no brain and smell like
>   a drain,
>
> But that doesn't matter to me.

The ewe responded:

> You may be a sheep, but I want you.
>
> My love is so deep and so real.
>
> You're ugly as sin and incredibly dim,
>
> But that doesn't change how I feel.

The ram began to hit himself repeatedly over the head with a stick.

'Why's he doing that?' Sid asked.

'He's trying to impress her,' Martin said. 'It's traditional. Let's go before he gets carried away.'

As soon as it grew dark, Martin suggested that they try and find a hotel.

'A hotel?' Sid asked.

'I hate sleeping outside,' said Martin. 'You could freeze to death or sleepwalk into a swamp or get torn apart by owls.'

Sid remembered his experience with the slugs from the night before. 'OK, but is there a hotel nearby?' he asked.

Martin nodded
and headed down
a hole, with Sid
clinging on more
tightly than ever.

At the bottom of the hole, an old
mole sat behind a wooden desk,
burping and eating nuts. 'Sorry, lads,
I'm full up,' he said.

As they headed back out of the
hole, Martin said to Sid, 'Don't worry,
I know somewhere else.'

He ran towards a hollow oak tree
and ducked inside. Sid and Martin
looked up and around. There were
lots of little ledges carved into the
hollow tree-trunk and on every ledge
an animal was asleep, covered with

a blanket of rushes
and with an acorn-
cup of water by their
heads. Sid saw
crickets, butterflies,
newts and weasels.

A hedgehog waddled over.
'No vacancies,' she said.

When they were back outside,
Martin said to Sid. 'We should have
booked in advance. Now we're as
good as dead.'

They set up camp under a clump
of toadstools.

'I hate sleeping
outside,'   said Martin.
                                'I know,'
                                said Sid.

But by now the two animals were so exhausted that they fell asleep almost at once.

Ten minutes later, they were surrounded by slugs. Hundreds of them slid smoothly through the grass. They formed a tight circle, three or four slugs deep, around the sleeping pair. Hundreds more joined them, black shapes glimmering dimly in the darkness.

They began to chant.

> Let's bash and mash and lash and gash
> and smash and slash and trash him.
> Let's crack and smack and whack and
> hack and thwack and all attack him.

When Sid woke up, he was already being dragged backwards through the grass by his tail. 'Martin,' he tried to shout, but nothing came out. More slugs climbed all over him. 'Martin!' he shouted, but Martin was still stretched out on his side, snoring. 'Martin!' Sid shouted again, and this time one of Martin's ears twitched.

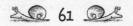

When Martin finally woke up, he saw a sea of black slugs and Sid bobbing up and down in the middle of them.

'Oh no,' Martin said. 'If there's one thing I hate more than bridges and onions and pelicans and small trees and tall trees, it's slugs.'

'Help!' Sid shouted. 'They're pulling my shell off!'

'OK, Sid, I'm coming,' shouted Martin with a frightened look on his face. He darted forwards and bit the nearest slug on the tail. 'Ew, sticky,' he said. He hit another slug on the head. 'Ew, slimy,' he said. He grabbed another slug by the tail and threw it out of the way. 'Ew, slithery,' he said.

But now there were more and more slugs and Sid was getting further and further away.

'I must be brave,' Martin said to himself. 'I must save my new friend.' He started flinging slugs about, left, right and centre. Sid's cries for help were growing fainter and fainter. Martin fought harder, kicking and punching with his paws, swiping and slashing with his tail. Sid fell silent and vanished underneath a thousand slugs. Martin put his head down and tried to charge through the black mass.

Just then, Martin heard the
beating of wings and the fluttering
of feathers. A dark shape swooped
down and knocked him sideways.
He looked up and saw a crow
standing in the middle of a patch
of grass, scooping up slugs with his
beak and swallowing them whole.

'Slugs are so tasty!' the crow
exclaimed.

He laid his head on the ground and used his wings to sweep more slugs into his beak. When the slugs tried to escape, he trod on them and said, 'Not so fast.' Within a few minutes, the clearing was empty, except for the crow, patting his stomach contentedly, and Sid the Snail looking up at him.

Martin scurried across the clearing and stood squarely in front of Sid.

'Excuse me, sir,' he said to the crow.
'I'm sorry to trouble you, but I was
wondering if you'd mind not eating
my friend.'

The crow looked down at Martin
and smiled. 'Of course I'm not going
to eat your friend. Crows don't eat
snails.'

'Don't they? Oh good,' said Martin.
'Er, how about mice?'

'No. Crows don't eat mice either,'
said the crow.

'Oh good,' said Martin.

The crow looked awkward and then said, 'Snails and mice don't eat crows, do they?'

'No,' said Sid and Martin.

'Excellent, then we're all friends. I'm Joe the Crow,' said the crow.

'I'm Sid the Snail,' said Sid.

'I'm Martin the Mouse,' said Martin.

Then, since it was the middle of the night, they all lay down behind an old tree stump and fell asleep.

Chapter Four

'So what brings you to these parts?' asked Joe the next day.

'We were just passing through,' said Sid, 'and we'd have kept going if we'd known there were so many slugs about.'

'Oh, there's no need to worry about them,' said Joe. 'I eat them for breakfast, dinner and tea.'

Martin grimaced at the thought.

'Where are you trying to get to?' Joe asked.

'The other end of the forest,' said Sid and Martin.

'That's where I'm going!' exclaimed Joe.

'We're going to find Ralph the Magic Rabbit,' said Sid.

'That's what I'm going to do!' exclaimed Joe.

Sid, Martin and Joe all looked surprised.

'Well, why don't we travel together?' said Joe. 'I get so bored on my own. It's been days since I've seen a friendly face.'

Sid looked at Martin and said, 'OK. But you realize we can't fly.'

'Oh, I'm happy to walk,' said Joe. 'To be honest, flying is highly overrated. Once you've seen one cloud, you've seen them all.'

Martin said, 'I've always disliked clouds. And heights. And travelling.'

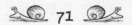 71

'So why are you both looking for Ralph the Magic Rabbit?' asked Joe.

'I want to be fast,' said Sid.

'I want to be strong,' said Martin.

'How about you?' asked Sid.

'I want to stand out,' said Joe.

'What do you mean?' Martin asked.

'Don't you stand out already?' Sid added, looking at Joe's sleek black feathers and sharp beak.

'I want Ralph the Magic Rabbit to make me multicoloured,' said Joe. 'You know, like a peacock or a parrot or a cockatoo. I've thought it all through. My tail feathers are going to be pink. My left wing's going to be blue. I'm going to have my chest done in yellow. And I'm going to have my right wing done in . . . sort of . . . cerise. You know, like cherry red. As for my head, I'm torn between –' he pulled a stack of leaves out from under his wing – 'this kind of green or maybe this kind of brown.'

Sid and Martin looked down at the leaves.

'I know. It's hard to decide, isn't it?' said Joe. 'The thing is, I've never felt like a crow inside. I'm supposed to perch on fence-posts and caw. I'm meant to be a harbinger of doom. But that's not really me, you know. I'm more of a happy-go-lucky, take-each-day-as-it-comes kind of bird. And if I don't feel like a crow, why should I look like a crow. That's the way I see it.'

Sid and Martin nodded and shook their heads.

'Things'll be a bit different round here when I'm multicoloured,' said Joe. 'I'll get invited to all the best parties. All the girl-crows will want to marry me. The younger crows will tell each other stories about my heroic feats.'

Sid and Martin were beginning to get restless.

'Shall we get going then?' said Martin.

'Let's find Ralph,' said Sid.

'Absolutely,' said Joe. As they set off he added, 'I'm so glad I met you two fine young fellows. Shall I sing us a song?'

'That's OK with me,' said Sid.

'As long as it's not scary,' said Martin.

Joe began to sing.

Oh, I love living in the wood.
The atmosphere is really good.
You should drop by, you really should
Next time you're in the
neighbourhood.

'Did you like it?' Joe asked.

'It wasn't terrible,' said Sid.

'Well, how about this one?' said Joe.

> I wish I was a puddle.
> It would be such fun
> Getting drunk by horses
> And dried out by the sun.

'It wasn't completely awful,' said Martin.

'I could teach those songbirds a thing or two,' said Joe. He hummed other songs to himself as they slowly travelled onwards.

79

Just before noon they reached the edge of a wide and misty marsh. Patches of grass and islands of moss poked out of the black and steaming mud. A sign on the left said:

THE SWAMP OF
~~CERTAIN DEATH~~
ETERNAL YOUTH

A water-snake's head emerged from the mud. 'Come and bathe in these magical waters,' the snake said, 'and you need never grow old.'

Another water-snake appeared.

'The years will simply fall away and you will be as a child again,' said the second snake.

'Those around you will wither and die while you remain fresh as a daisy,' the first snake said.

'Just five minutes in the swamp,' the second snake said, 'and time will no longer have any meaning.'

The two snakes sank back into the mud.

'Now, I usually give everyone the benefit of the doubt,' said Joe, 'but I didn't like those snakes at all.'

'Is that a cow's leg sticking up over there?' asked Martin.

'There's something wrong with

that sign,' said Sid, 'but I can't quite figure out what.'

A strange groaning noise came from beneath the mud.

'So are we all agreed,' said Sid, 'that we walk around this swamp?'

'Absolutely,' said Martin.

'Good idea,' said Joe.

After half an hour of walking, and trying to ignore the hissing and bubbling, they didn't seem to have got very far.

'The swamp is wider than we thought,' said Martin. 'This is going to take us ages.'

'I hope I'm not wearing you out,' said Sid as he clung to Martin's fur.

'It's a shame you two can't fly,' said Joe, 'because we could just leap over this swamp –' Joe stopped all of a sudden. 'Hang on a minute! I could teach you!'

Sid looked down at Martin, who looked up at Sid.

'It's very easy,' said Joe. 'I realize it's not exactly fun, there's not much to do up there, but it does come in handy in situations like this.'

'I'm sorry, Joe, I couldn't,' said Martin.

Sid looked up at the sky. 'It's going to get dark soon, Martin,' he said.

Martin looked over at the swamp and then over at Joe. He sighed. 'What have you got in mind?'

'That's the spirit,' said Joe. 'Now, you two stand over there.'

Martin went and stood about ten paces away from Joe. Sid got off Martin's back.

'Now flap your arms as fast as you can,' said Joe.

Martin flapped his arms rapidly. Sid stared at Joe. 'What am I supposed to flap?' he asked.

'Flap your feelers,' Joe said. 'Now raise your tails.'

Martin and Sid flapped and raised their tails.

'Now push down with your feet,' Joe said.

Martin and Sid pushed down on the ground.

'Lift up your heads,' Joe said.

They lifted up their heads.

'And fly,' said Joe.

Martin and Sid stayed rooted to the spot, flapping, raising their tails, pushing down on the ground and lifting their heads.

'Good effort,' said Joe.

Martin and Sid ran out of breath and stopped.

'The thing is, we've not got much time,' said Joe. 'If only there was another way of getting across this swamp.' His eyes lit up. 'Of course!'

'What?' said Martin.

'Have you ever ridden on a frog before?' Joe asked.

'You what?' replied Sid.

'My friend Alfonso lives round here. Alfonso!'

A few seconds passed and a large green frog hopped towards them.

'Al, old pal!' exclaimed Joe.

Alfonso's reply was slow, because every once in a while he would spot a fly, shoot his long tongue out, catch the fly and swallow it.

87

'Hello, Joe,' he said, 'it's been a (gulp) while since I've seen you. What have you (gulp) been up to?'

'Oh, this and that,' said Joe. 'Listen, Alfonso, I need a favour. Can you give my friend here a lift across this swamp?'

'I'd be (gulp) delighted and –' Alfonso began to cough violently. 'Sorry, a gnat went down the wrong way.'

'Bleurgh, I hate that,' said Joe.

'Pop your (gulp) friend on my back and we'll (gulp) get going,' said Alfonso.

Joe the Crow lifted Sid up by his shell

and placed him gently on Alfonso's
back.

'Just a second –' said Sid. But
Alfonso was already bounding over
the marsh, landing only on the firm
and dry patches, avoiding the
stagnant pools and murky holes.

Joe and Martin watched Sid
disappear into the mist.

'Now what?' asked Martin.

'I have something else in mind for you,' said Joe. 'Meet me at the top of that tree.'

He pointed to a giant cedar tree next to the swamp.

'Bu-but –' squeaked Martin, 'what if I fall out? What if it falls down? What if I get stuck up there?'

'You'll be all right,' said Joe and took off.

Martin hesitated for a moment, but quickly realized he was on his own and it was getting dark.

As he scrambled up the tree, he said to himself, 'After I find Ralph the Magic Rabbit, I'll be as strong as an ox, as deadly as a rattlesnake and as

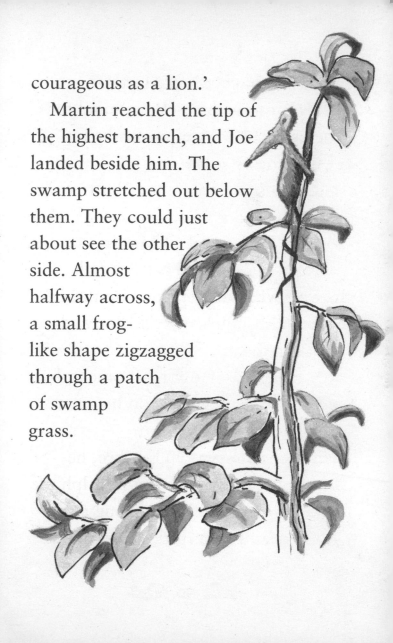

courageous as a lion.'

Martin reached the tip of the highest branch, and Joe landed beside him. The swamp stretched out below them. They could just about see the other side. Almost halfway across, a small frog-like shape zigzagged through a patch of swamp grass.

'Have you ever been leaf-gliding before?' Joe asked.

'Leaf what?' Martin asked.

'Oh, you're really going to like this,' said Joe.

He plucked a leaf from the tree with his beak and passed it to Martin.

'Now, you have to hold the leaf high above your head and leap off the end of the branch,' said Joe. 'Once you're in the air, you steer by tilting it up, down, left or right.'

Martin was speechless.

'Aim for the oak tree on the other side of the swamp. We'll all meet there,' said Joe.

'W-w-wait,' said Martin.

'Once we're over there, we can find

some dinner,' said Joe. He smiled and flew away.

The wind began to whistle and the tree rocked back and forth. Martin whimpered. He slowly raised the leaf above his head. Just as he had decided not to do it, the wind picked him up and lifted him into the air.

Sid and Joe were on the other side of the swamp, watching Martin being blown up and down, to and fro.

'He must be enjoying it,' Joe said, 'he's been up there for ages.'

When Martin finally landed, his leaf was in tatters. He lay on the ground, staring blankly into space.

'Don't be sad,' Joe said cheerfully. 'You can have another go tomorrow.'

Chapter Five

The following morning, Sid couldn't stop talking about his ride on Alfonso's back: 'And then we jumped over a rock, and then we changed direction in mid-air, and then we raced past all those snakes.'

Finally Sid said to Martin, 'Was leaf-gliding fun too?'

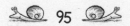

But Martin didn't say a word; he just looked down at his feet. As they set off on their journey again, Martin started to sing quietly.

When things are going badly,
    run away.
In times of crisis, leave without delay.
Don't stay and fight it out.
You'll die without a doubt.
When things are going badly,
    run away.

When it's time to save the day,
   forget it.
When your courage slips away,
   just let it.
Don't try to be a hero
Cos survival rates are zero.
So when it's time to save the day,
   forget it.

If someone asks for help,
   just step aside.
When you're badly needed,
   run and hide.
Don't risk an early grave
Pretending to be brave.
When someone asks for help,
   just step aside.

Martin sang the song through twice, then fell silent again. Sid looked over at Joe.

'What part of the forest are you from?' he asked.

'Oh, I'm not from this forest,' said Joe.

'Not from this forest,' exclaimed Sid, and his feelers twirled around. 'You mean there are others?'

'Oh yes, lots of others,' said Joe. 'I'll give you a tour of them after we've found Ralph the Magic Rabbit.'

'So-so wh-what was your forest like?' Sid stammered.

'Oh, not as nice as this. More trees, fewer fields. But then Ralph the Magic Rabbit lives here; he's not going to choose a dump, is he?' Joe paused and scratched his back with his wing.

'Still, my favourite is the forest about eight miles from here,' Joe went on. 'If you fly to the western edge, you reach the sea. You can sit in the top of a tree, watching the dolphins leaping around and seals' heads popping up above the waves.'

Sid was speechless with wonder.

* * *

At about eleven o'clock Sid told Joe
he was getting hungry.

Joe said, 'Are you? Well, there must
be a cafe round here somewhere.'
He hopped over to a
hollow tree-trunk
and peered inside.

A mouse was sitting on a chair,
while a crab cut his fur. Snip, snip,

went the crab's pincers. A duck
and a ferret sat on pebbles nearby,
waiting their turn. A sign was carved
into the trunk: COLIN THE CRAB'S
CUT-PRICE CUTS.

'No,' said Joe.

He strolled over to a hole in the side of a hillock and squeezed himself inside. Behind a desk there was a snowy owl with a stethoscope round his neck.

'Sit down, sit down,' the owl said. 'Now let's have a look at you. Hmm, I can see why you're here. Crooked beak, shabby feathers, stiff knees. Good job we've caught it early.'

'Actually, I was looking for a cafe,' said Joe.

'Oh,' said the owl. 'Try the bush opposite.'

Joe squeezed back out of the hole and fluttered towards a small brown bush.

'Sid, Martin, over here,' he said. They crept slowly into the bush. Sid crept forwards too until Martin said, 'Sid, you're standing on my nose.'

As they got closer to the middle of the bush they began to hear music and conversation. They took a few more steps and saw lots of animals sitting round small stone tables on short wooden stools. On the left there was a bar, behind which two weasels in bow ties served the drinks. On the right, a snail was on the top of a mound, singing.

When your shell is far too heavy
And you're sick of eating plants,
Don't shout and throw your
    weight about.
Get on your feet and dance!

'This place is great!' said Sid.

Sid, Joe and Martin sat at an empty table.

A weasel in a bow tie appeared to take their order.

'What food do you do?' Joe asked.

'Worms, caterpillars, grass, flowers and mushrooms,' said the weasel.

'No slugs?' Joe asked, looking disappointed.

'Sorry, they escaped,' said the weasel.

'Give us half a dozen
caterpillars then,' said Joe.

'What do I get if I order flowers?'
Sid asked.

'Er, sort of a small bouquet,' the
weasel said, 'mainly blues and pinks.'

'Sounds delicious,' said Sid.

'What are you having then,
Martin?' Joe asked.

'Nothing,' mumbled Martin.

'Are you feeling a bit down?' Sid asked.

Martin shrugged.

'And nothing for the squeaker,' the weasel said, and left them alone.

While they were waiting for their food, Sid looked around. They were right in the middle of the bush. A tangle of branches and leaves arched over their heads and formed the roof of the cafe.

'What was that?' Martin said.

'What was what?' Sid replied.

'That noise,' said Martin, flicking his ears back.

Now Sid could hear it too. It sounded like the rumbling of thunder.

The ground began to tremble and everything in the cafe started to shake. Two squirrels ran into the cafe at the same time. They both started to speak at once, then both stopped.

'After you, dear boy,' said the first squirrel.

'No, after you,' said the second squirrel.

'No, no, Tarquin, I absolutely insist,' said the first.

'Please, Terence, you are the superior orator,' said the second.

'Very well,' said the first, and cleared his throat.

This caused panic in the cafe. Animals hid under tables and behind chairs. They clambered over each other; they shoved past each other. Some called for help and some barked out orders. In the meantime, the pounding was getting louder and louder.

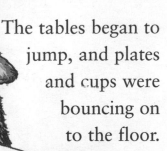

The tables began to jump, and plates and cups were bouncing on to the floor.

'I was beginning to think that this trip couldn't get any worse,' said Martin. 'How wrong I was. If we survive this, you know what's next, don't you? We'll be ambushed by foxes and buried in a hole, so they can eat us later. Then we'll be dug up by wolves and torn limb from limb. Then we'll be carried off by eagles and pecked to death.'

The trembling had turned into an earthquake. Everyone in the cafe was being thrown up and down as if they were on a trampoline. Only Sid and the other snail clung tightly to the earth. They were rippling like ribbons.

The noise was deafening. The cafe was falling to pieces, everybody was screaming, but all anyone could hear was the drumming and drubbing of horse's hoofs.

The horses rushed by and the bush leaned after them.

Now nobody could see anything either. Sid tried to keep his eyes open as things shook and shook and became more and more blurred until they melted into each other.

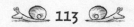

As the noise began to recede, the tables in the cafe slowly settled back on to the floor. Everything in the room gradually came back into focus.

'Martin? Joe?' Sid murmured.

The pounding of hoofs was a distant sound again. Sid looked around and saw upside-down stools, tables on their sides and broken acorn-cups and tree-bark plates.

He could vaguely make out the other snail on the far side of the cafe.

'Hello!' Sid shouted.

But the snail had been knocked out by a pebble.

Sid began to move through the wreckage. He couldn't see or hear anyone, though they wouldn't have had time to get very far. He looked for a trail left by Martin's paws or Joe's claws, but there was nothing.

'Up here!' someone said.
Sid looked up and saw,
in the canopy of leaves
and branches above the
cafe, dozens of animals
wedged tightly into
place and unable to move.
There were birds and
mammals and insects.
Some were buried deep inside the
shrubbery; others were dangling
by an arm or wing.

'Sid,' someone called.

'Martin,' Sid answered.

He looked up and saw
Martin trapped behind
a gnarled and
knotted branch.

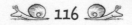

'I can't move,' said Martin.

'Hang on,' said Sid, 'I'll see if I can get you down.'

Sid rummaged around and picked up a small stone with one of his feelers.

'I'm going to try to dislodge you,' said Sid.

'OK,' said Martin.

Sid threw the stone. It hit Martin on the nose.

'Ow,' said Martin.

'Sorry,' said Sid.

Martin said, 'Try to find a stick; then I can use it to climb down.'

'OK,' said Sid.

He looked for a stick that was long enough to reach the cafe roof. As he searched, he heard moaning and groaning above him. 'I told you we should have gone somewhere else,' said one voice. 'Your foot is in my eye,' said another.

Sid crawled towards a suitably long branch and tried to lift it. He struggled and strained and managed to hold it above his head. He swung it up towards Martin. He twisted it and shook it and it seemed to hold fast.

'OK, try to climb down,' said Sid.

There was no reply.

'Martin,' said Sid.

There was still nothing.

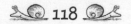

Finally, Martin replied in a muffled voice, 'You've pushed me further into the bush.'

'Whoops, sorry,' said Sid, and pulled the stick back down.

As Sid tried to think of another plan, he heard someone singing from deep inside the bush. It could only have been Joe.

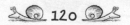

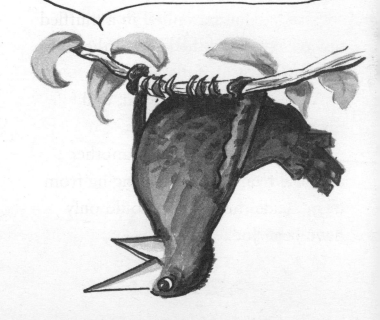

The whole bush came to life. 'Shut up!' shouted one voice. 'Will you be quiet?' yelled another. 'What a dreadful voice!' cried a third. But Sid was happier now he knew that Joe was all right. He tried to think of other ways to rescue everyone from the roof. He headed over to the bar. He was about to climb up on to it when he saw something glinting on the floor. It had obviously fallen off the bar. As he crawled towards it, he heard Joe's voice again. 'Well, I'm sorry you didn't like my song but, don't worry, I have plenty of others.' 'No!' thundered everyone else in the bush. 'Has anyone heard "The Ballad of Barry the Bad-Tempered Badger"?' Joe asked.

'Yes!' everyone else shouted.

Sid picked up the glinting object and saw that it was a small brown-and-white shell. There was a piece of bark tied to it and, on the bark, this message had been written: IN EMERGENCIES, PLEASE BLOW. For a split second Sid thought, Does this count as a real emergency? Will I get into trouble? Then he heard a voice above him saying, 'Listen, crow, if you sing another note, I'm going to crawl through this bush and shut you up once and for all!'

Sid put the shell to his lips and blew.

There were a few seconds of silence.
Then the animals trapped in the bush
began to mutter, 'Was that a horn?
Did someone blow the horn?' Then
silence again.

Sid waited a few seconds and
considered blowing the horn for a
second time. As he put the shell to
his lips, hundreds of ants poured into
the cafe. They were carrying sticks,

rocks, leaves, acorn-cups full of water,
shells, flowers, lumps of moss and
ears of wheat. They all seemed to be
talking at once: 'Over here! Down
there! Take this! Give me that!' One
of the ants came up to Sid and said,
'Well done, son, but you can leave
the rest to us.'

The army of ants began their rescue work. They used long sticks to dislodge the animals hanging from the roof, catching them in large, stretched-out leaves. Twenty or thirty ants formed a ladder by balancing on each other's shoulders.

The ant at the top of the ladder disappeared into the bush and reappeared with a confused-looking sparrow. Six ants walked past Sid and returned a few seconds later carrying a weasel. Other ants replaced the chairs and tables and cleared away the debris.

Sid watched as they pulled Martin, and then Joe, out of the roof. He breathed a huge sigh of relief and headed over to his friends.

Chapter Six

Joe, Martin and Sid were back on the road again.

'Well done, Sid. You saved us from a nasty scrape back there,' said Joe.

'Yes, thank you, Sid,' said Martin. 'I thought I was going to die of starvation.'

'Oh, I didn't do anything really,' said Sid.

'Of course you did,' said Joe. 'You blew the horn, didn't you?'

'If those ants hadn't come,' said Martin, 'that bush would have been full of skeletons.'

Sid said, 'Yes, but –' and then stopped. He smiled, looked at Joe and Martin and said, 'I'm glad I was able to help.'

Joe led the way along a forest path, closely followed by Martin, with Sid still clinging on to his fur.

'You know what,' Joe said after a while. 'I think we're nearly there.'

'Thank goodness for that,' said Martin with a deep sigh. 'Another day like this would finish me off.'

'I'll just find out if we're on the right track,' Joe said.

They were in a small forest clearing surrounded by ash trees. At the bottom of one of these trees Joe saw a hedgehog rolled up into a ball.

The sides of the ball were moving in and out, and a loud snoring noise came from somewhere inside it. Joe marched cheerfully up to the ball,

while Martin and Sid followed him
tentatively.

'Hello!' Joe exclaimed.

The hedgehog instantly unrolled
himself and spluttered, 'What the
devil?'

'Hello!' said Joe. 'We were just
passing by and we thought we'd
say hello.'

The hedgehog looked furious.
'You birdbrain! You feather-head!
I was fast asleep!'

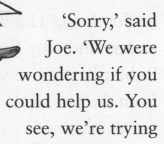

'Sorry,' said Joe. 'We were wondering if you could help us. You see, we're trying to find Ralph the Magic Rabbit.'

This stopped the hedgehog dead in his tracks. 'Ralph the Magic Rabbit? But that's where I'm going. I was just having a rest because I've been walking all night,' he said.

'Well, what a coincidence,' said Joe. 'I'm Joe the Crow. Pleased to meet you.'

'I'm Hugo the Hedgehog,' said the hedgehog.

'Have you been travelling long?' Joe asked.

'Too long,' Hugo said. 'I fail to understand why Ralph the Magic Rabbit has to live so bloomin' far from the rest of the world.'

'What are you going to ask him for?' Joe asked.

Hugo looked awkward and raised his bushy eyebrows. 'I want to be (ahem) fluffy,' he said.

Joe stammered, 'Wh-what?'

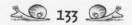

'Have you any idea how hard it is having bristles?' Hugo asked. 'You can't walk across a field without accidentally stabbing someone. Every time I wash my back, my paws are cut to ribbons. This is why I want to be (ahem) fluffy – like a squirrel or a sheep. Nobody fears for their life when a sheep comes towards them.'

'I see what you mean,' said Joe.

'I'm going to be the fluffiest creature in the world,' said Hugo. 'Like a giant cloud.'

Joe told Hugo that Ralph the Magic Rabbit was going to make him multicoloured. He introduced Sid and Martin. 'Hugo is after Ralph the Magic Rabbit as well,' Joe said. 'He's going to show us the way.'

Hugo looked at Sid balancing on Martin's back. 'I'd offer you a lift,' he said, 'but you'd be torn to shreds.'

Hugo led them through a shady thicket into dense undergrowth.

'Ow,' said Martin as he inadvertently bumped into Hugo.

'Sorry,' said Hugo.

'I'm blind, I'm blind,' protested Martin.

Hugo walked through a patch of nettles and down a grassy bank.

'Now, if my information is correct,' Hugo said, 'it should be just over there.'

There was one final row of trees, then nothing; just miles and miles of level plains, as far as the eye could see. Behind them, the forest with its bushes and ponds and ditches and birds and insects. In front of them, just empty fields stretching away to the horizon.

'The end of the forest,' whispered Sid.

'And look,' said Hugo.

In front of them, in the middle of this flat and featureless expanse, there was a single, solitary hill. It was five metres high and covered in grass.

At the bottom of the hill there were two doors, one on the left and one on the right. In front of each door there was a long queue of animals – although the queue on the right was much longer. In front of the hill, in between these two doors, there was a whiskery old rabbit shouting and pointing.

'We did it,' said Martin.

The four animals made their way
over to the large mound.

'The world and his wife are here,'
growled Hugo. 'Have they got
nothing better to do?'

As they approached the hill, the
whiskery old rabbit came towards
them.

'Which queue do you need?' he asked.

Hugo, Joe, Martin and Sid all looked at each other blankly.

'We don't know,' said Joe.

The rabbit sighed impatiently. 'What are you here for?' he asked.

They explained that they wanted to be fast, strong, colourful and fluffy.

'The queue on the left,' the rabbit barked.

Hugo, Joe, Martin and Sid went to join the left-hand queue.

'That's good,' Sid said to Martin, 'because the queue on the right is longer.'

The four animals joined the back of the queue. Within thirty seconds, three more animals had joined. Within two minutes, there were fifteen animals behind them. Another minute passed and there was a massive assortment of woodland creatures behind them, all chattering and jostling.

There were two small voles in front of them in the queue.

'Hello, I'm Joe the Crow,' said Joe. 'Pleased to meet you. What are you here for?'

'We want to be huge,' said the first vole.

'Then we won't get eaten by owls,' said the second.

In front of the voles, eight or nine bluebottles were hovering.

'Hello, I'm Joe the Crow,' said Joe. 'What are you here for?'

'We want a sting,' said one.

'Like a wasp or a bee,' said another.

Behind him in the queue, Joe discovered a spider who wanted wings, a bat who wanted to see properly and a duck who thought he was in the queue for the post office and who promptly left.

In the meantime, Hugo, Joe, Sid and Martin were getting closer to the front of the queue. Sid felt increasingly nervous. He had come so far and seen so much, and now his journey was over. He couldn't believe he was about to meet Ralph the Magic Rabbit. Half of him wanted to jump for joy and half of him wanted to run away.

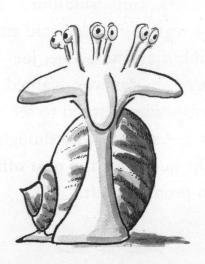

'Are you all right?' said a voice by his side. It was Joe.

'A bit anxious,' said Sid.

'Me too,' said Joe.

'You too!' exclaimed Sid.

'I've been dreaming of this for years,' said Joe. 'I never thought I'd actually do it.'

Sid thought for a few seconds and said, 'I still don't understand why you didn't fly here. You could have arrived ages ago.'

Joe smiled and said, 'I couldn't have done this on my own. I needed company. I needed to be with friends.'

Sid thought about this for a while. He knew what Joe meant.

'OK, those two voles are going in, then it's us,' said Hugo.

Martin began to panic. 'What if Ralph the Magic Rabbit isn't in there? What if it's a monster?'

'We'd better sort ourselves out,' said Hugo. 'Smallest first. That means you, Sid.'

Sid began to protest, but Joe and Martin agreed: 'Smallest first.'

The two voles went in and the whiskery old rabbit cried out, 'Next.'

Martin walked towards the door
with Sid on his back. Sid slid down on
to the floor. He looked up at the door
and then back at Joe, Martin and
Hugo.

The door opened, the whiskery old
rabbit shouted, 'Enter,'
and Sid went in.

When the door closed behind him,
Sid found himself in total darkness.
He looked left and right, up and down

but couldn't see a thing. He didn't know what he was supposed to do next. He could smell the earth underneath him and the damp air around him.

Suddenly there was colour everywhere. He was in the middle of a huge cavern, surrounded by bright and beautiful objects. On his left, there were orange carrots, yellow daffodils, white seashells and dark brown conkers.

On his right, there were green apples, blue quartz crystals, golden honeycombs and black seaweed. In the middle of all this, sitting on a mound with his legs crossed, was Ralph the Magic Rabbit.

'What? How?' Sid stammered.

'How did you get here?' Ralph said. 'Oh, that was easy enough.'

Ralph clicked his fingers. Sid was hanging upside down from the ceiling.

Click! Sid was at the top of a tree in the middle of the forest.

Click! Sid was floating on an iceberg in the Antarctic Ocean.

Click! Sid was back in front of Ralph the Magic Rabbit again.

'What is your name, snail?' Ralph asked.

'Sid,' said Sid.

'Sid? Is that all? Mine is Ralph Hubert Montgomery Charles. It's because I'm so important, you see.'

'I do see, yes,' said Sid nervously.

'And how old are you, Sid?' Ralph asked.

'I don't know,' said Sid. 'About two, I think.'

'I'm a hundred and six. A hundred and seven next Thursday,' said Ralph. 'It seems like only yesterday that I was eighty-seven.'

'H-Happy Birthday,' stammered Sid.

'So what can I do for you, Sid?'
Ralph asked.

Sid could not believe that the
moment had arrived. He swallowed
hard.

'Come on, come on,' said Ralph, 'what are you here for?'

Sid said, 'Please, Ralph the Magic Rabbit, sir, if it's not too much trouble, I would like to be . . . fast.'

'Fast? That's no problem at all. What would you like to be? A cheetah? A gazelle? An eagle swooping through the sky?'

'No, no,' said Sid, 'I still want to be a snail, just a fast one.'

'But that's impossible,' Ralph replied. 'Have you ever seen a snail racing through the fields at seventy miles per hour? No, no, I can only turn you into a fast animal. I can't break the laws of nature.'

'But – I – don't –' Sid mumbled.

'Come on, do you really enjoy being a snail?' asked Ralph. 'Taking ages to get everywhere? Getting accosted by slugs?'

Sid thought about this carefully.
He actually quite liked being a snail.
Thanks to Martin, it hadn't taken him
long to get across the forest. Thanks
to Joe, the slugs had left him alone.

'I'm sorry, but I'm going to have to
hurry you,' said Ralph. 'What about
being a dolphin? They're pretty fast.'

Sid pictured being a dolphin, swerving through the rocks and reeds. He stared at Ralph's feet and said blankly, 'I want to carry on being a snail.'

'Very well,' said Ralph. He clicked his fingers and Sid found himself back on the edge of the forest, staring at the huge mound with two doors and two queues.

Now Sid was hit by a huge wave of regret. He had finally found Ralph the Magic Rabbit. He could have been a cheetah or an eagle or a dolphin. He had chosen to continue being a snail. He should join the back of the queue and ask Ralph the Magic Rabbit again. He wouldn't make the same mistake twice.

But as he began to move he asked himself, did he really want to be a dolphin? Getting chased by sharks?

He liked his shell and his feelers and the slimy trail he made in the grass.

He began to wonder what had happened to Martin and Joe and Hugo. At that moment, he saw a mouse nosing its way through the grass towards him.

'Martin!' he exclaimed.

'Sid!' Martin said. 'You're still you!'

'You're still you too,' said Sid.

'I wanted to be strong,' said Martin, 'but I didn't want to be a rhino or an elephant or a bear. Come on, climb on my back and we'll find Joe.'

Martin, with Sid hanging on, scuttled back towards the mound. They approached the whiskery old rabbit.

'Shall we ask him?' asked Martin.

'Ask him what?' Sid replied.

'If he's seen a crow,' Martin said.

'But what if Joe's not a crow any

more,' Sid said. 'What if he's a peacock or a parrot?'

They heard a fluttering sound and Joe landed beside them.

'Joe!' exclaimed Sid. 'You're still you!'

'You're both still you too,' said Joe.

'We thought you might have . . .' said Martin.

'No way,' said Joe 'I wanted to be colourful, but he threatened to turn me into a budgerigar. I said to him, "Can't you just turn me into a multicoloured crow?" He said no. I said, "You're supposed to have magical powers. You're not very magical if you can't even dye my feathers a different colour." Next thing I know, I'm out here, flapping around in mid-air.'

Sid and Martin smiled broadly. Then the whiskery old rabbit came up to them, 'Which queue do you want? Left or right?' he asked.

'Neither, thanks,' said Joe.

'Out of interest, what is

the queue on the right for?' Sid asked.

'The queue on the left is for those who want to be turned into a different animal,' said the rabbit. 'The queue on the right is for those who have been turned into a different animal and who now want to be turned back.'

Sid, Joe and Martin looked at the right-hand queue. It stretched back as far as the eye could see, and it was getting longer all the time.

Joe looked down at Martin and Sid. 'Come on, let's go home,' he said.

They walked back towards the forest. They were all thinking hard about what had just happened and what they had done. Even Joe didn't feel like making conversation.

They had just reached the edge of the forest when they heard someone shouting behind them.

'Sid! Martin! Joe!'

Sid, Martin and Joe turned round. They watched as a wolf cub bounded towards them, laughing and panting.

'It's me!' the cub said. 'Hugo the Hedgehog!'

'Hugo?' Joe, Martin and Sid all exclaimed.

'Yes!' Hugo said as he reached them. 'Look at all this beautiful fur. Go on, stroke me, I know you want to.'

'We're fine, thanks,' said Sid.

'But how come you're all still the same? Didn't you get to see Ralph the Magic Rabbit?' Hugo asked.

'Yes we did, but –' Martin began.

'Oh, I see,' said Hugo, 'you decided against it. Well, I'm over the moon. No more prickles. No more spikes. Just lovely warm fur.'

He opened his mouth, looked up at the sky and barked cheerfully, 'Ow-ow-owwwwww. Now I'm going to show all my friends,' he added, and he bounded into the undergrowth and out of sight. Joe, Martin and Sid all looked at each other.

'Good luck to him,' Joe said.

'He's going to need it,' said Martin.

* * *

The three animals walked slowly back through the forest.

'Which way are you going?' Joe asked.

'I don't know,' said Sid.

'Which way are you going?' asked Martin.

'Have you ever heard of Al the All-Powerful Cow?' Joe asked.

'No!' exclaimed Sid and Martin.

'Apparently she's like Ralph the Magic Rabbit, only better,' said Joe.

'Where does she live?' Sid asked.

'A hundred and one miles away,' said Joe.

There was a brief pause.

'It sounds an awfully long way,' said Sid.

'Cows are fierce predators who hunt in packs and attack without warning,' said Martin.

'Oh come on, it'll be fun,' said Joe. 'And, besides, what else have you got to do?'

Sid and Martin looked at each other.

'All right,' said Sid.

'OK,' said Martin.

'Off we go then,' said Joe.